c Dd Ee

h Ii Jj Kk

Oo Pp Qq

Uu Vv

Yy Zz

This alphabet was inspired by original paintings of Luke's children and by the woodcuts of William Nicholson. As in traditional alphabets, every letter is illustrated by a simple object or action. Running alongside, Kate's poem takes a less literal approach, responding to the mood of each picture in a loosely rhymed celebration of childhood.

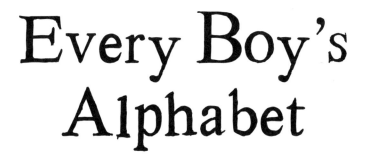

# Every Boy's Alphabet

Kate Bingham  Luke Martineau

GRAFFEG

Every boy is an action hero.

Every boy is as big as his boots.

Every boy loves to tumble
and clown.

Drummer boys don't
follow suit.

Every boy needs extra energy.

Every boy can think
with his feet.

Every boy comes and goes
as he pleases.

Every boy hates holding hands
in the street.

No boy is an island.

Every boy wants job
satisfaction,

someone he can surprise
with kindness,

somewhere to learn
without distraction.

Every monkey gets
up to mischief.

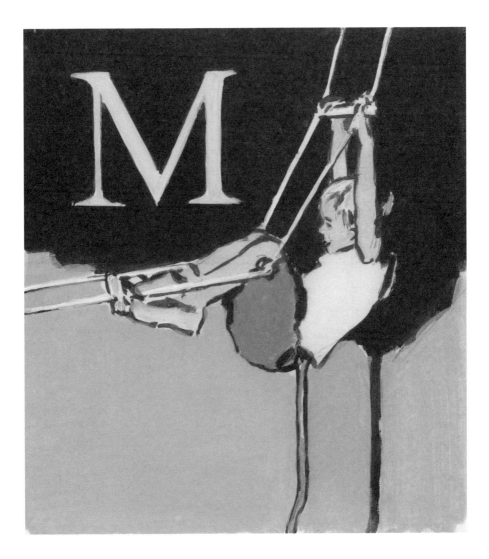

Nature-lovers know to wait.

# Every young Odysseus

has perilous seas to navigate.

Some boys respond to
quick-fire questions,

other boys need time
for reflection.

Every boy is a shooting star.

Every toy wants close
inspection.

Every boy looks up
to the universe.

Every voyager thinks of home.

Every boy is a wonder
to watch.

Extroverts expose their bones.

Dreamers yo-yo to the moon.

Every boy needs zzz to zoom.

# Every Boy's Alphabet

Every boy is an action hero.
Every boy is as big as his boots.
Every boy loves to tumble and clown.
Drummer boys don't follow suit.
Every boy needs extra energy.
Every boy can think with his feet.
Every boy comes and goes as he pleases.
Every boy hates holding hands in the street.
No boy is an island.
Every boy wants job satisfaction,
someone he can surprise with kindness,
somewhere to learn without distraction.
Every monkey gets up to mischief.
Nature-lovers know to wait.
Every young Odysseus
has perilous seas to navigate.
Some boys respond to quick-fire questions,
other boys need time for reflection.
Every boy is a shooting star.
Every toy wants close inspection.
Every boy looks up to the universe.
Every voyager thinks of home.
Every boy is a wonder to watch.
Extroverts expose their bones.
Dreamers yo-yo to the moon.
Every boy needs zzz to zoom.

Adventurous, daring, curious, caring: there is something of every girl in this delightful alphabet character, who jumps for joy *and* learns to keep her feet on the ground. The affection visible in Luke Martineau's fluid illustrations is matched by Kate Bingham's tender, witty poem, written to appeal to adults as much as to the puzzling younger mind.

Available from all good bookshops and
online at www.graffeg.com

# About the authors

**Kate Bingham** has published two novels and three books of poetry: *Cohabitation, Quicksand Beach* and *Infragreen*. She was shortlisted for the Forward Prize in 2006 and 2010, and her newest poems can sometimes be found in the TLS and the Spectator. Read more about her work at katebingham.com.

**Luke Martineau** is a painter of informal family portraits, landscapes and still life. For 25 years he has exhibited in London, where he lives. When not drawing inspiration from his own family, painting trips have taken him to Sweden, Germany, Italy, the US, Cambodia, Hong Kong and India. He is currently President of Chelsea Art Society. See more about Luke at lukemartineau.com.

Luke and Kate have been friends since they were students, and this collaboration has grown in step with their own children, some of whom are now students themselves.

**Kate Holland** is a multi-award winning bookbinder, specialising in contemporary fine binding to commission. Her books are held in the collections of the British, Bodleian and Yale University Libraries, amongst others. Much of the design, layout and typesetting of this book is her work. Limited editions, signed by the authors, are available at kateholландbooks.co.uk.

Every Boy's Alphabet
Published in Great Britain in 2018
by Graffeg Limited.

Written by Kate Bingham
copyright © 2017. Illustrated by Luke
Martineau copyright © 2017. Designed by
Kate Holland © 2017. Designed and produced
by Graffeg Limited copyright © 2018.

Graffeg Limited, 24 Stradey Park Business
Centre, Mwrwg Road, Llangennech, Llanelli,
Carmarthenshire SA14 8YP Wales UK
Tel 01554 824000  www.graffeg.com

ISBN 9781912654543

1 2 3 4 5 6 7 8 9

Aa Bb C

Ff Gg H

Ll Mm N

Rr Ss T

Ww X